D0119234

Jane Yolen

WHAT TO DO WITH A STICK

illustrated by
Paolo Domeniconi

designed by Rita Marshall

Creative Editions

A stick! A stick!
A remarkable toy.
It can bring you much magic
and also much joy.

A stick is a sword
to tame monsters of dread.

Or bend it to use as a
large bow instead.

It can anchor a ship.

It can hold down a pulley.

A stick draws the line
between you and a bully.

Like a seal, you can balance
a stick on your nose.

It can help when you're crossing cold Arctic ice floes.

You can throw out your stick
to a big polar bear.
He will fetch it right back
without turning a hair.

(If... you... dare!)

You can use a long stick
to fish for brown trout,
or fix up a weather vane
spinning about.

As an oar for a rowboat
in puddle or pond.

Or used for a spell
as a wizard's wild wand.

You can ride on a stick
like a witch in full sail.

Or hold up a flag
so it waves in a gale.

It can serve as propeller
on any biplane

flying to London
or possibly Spain.

A stick! A stick's
a remarkable thing,
though to give it more *oomph*,
and to make your heart sing...

Go find a strong box and a possible string.

And make music that goes
with ... everything!

Text copyright © 2023 by Jane Yolen   Illustrations copyright © 2023 by Paolo Domeniconi

Edited by Kate Riggs   Published in 2023 by Creative Editions

P.O. Box 227, Mankato, MN 56002 USA

Creative Editions is an imprint of The Creative Company

www.thecreativecompany.us

All rights reserved. No part of the contents of this book may be reproduced
by any means without the written permission of the publisher. Printed in China

Library of Congress Cataloging-in-Publication Data

Names: Yolen, Jane, author. I Domeniconi, Paolo, illustrator.

Title: What to do with a stick / by Jane Yolen; illustrated by Paolo Domeniconi.

Summary: Illustrations and rhyming text celebrate the remarkable joys of
a stick that can anchor a daydream, fend off monsters, and even make music.

Identifiers: LCCN 2022001847 (print) I LCCN 2022001848 (ebook)

ISBN 9781568463650 (hardcover) I ISBN 9781682772850 (paperback) I ISBN 9781640007567 (ebook)

Subjects: CYAC: Stories in rhyme. I Staffs (Sticks, canes, etc.)—Fiction.

I Imagination—Fiction. I Play—Fiction. I LCGFT: Picture books. I Stories in rhyme.

Classification: LCC PZ8.3.Y76 Wgk 2023 (print) I LCC PZ8.3.Y76 (ebook) I DDC [E]—dc23

LC record available at https://lccn.loc.gov/2022001847

LC ebook record available at https://lccn.loc.gov/2022001848

Printed in China

9 8 7 6 5 4 3 2